The Bon Air Boys Adventures

THE SECRET OF HICKORY HILL

BY

GREG W. GOLDEN

Carson | Knight Publishing
All Rights Reserved
Mobile, Alabama

From Carson | Knight Publishing, 2019

PRINTED IN THE UNITED STATES OF AMERICA

ACKNOWLEDGEMENTS

The Bon Air Boys Adventure book series was birthed during the innocence of a simpler time. When my dad flicked on the porch light of our house once the summer sun had set, that was my cue to tell my buddies goodnight and head home for a much-dreaded bath. We played hard and long in my neighborhood.

My formative years unfolded within a dozen, peaceful square blocks in mid-America. Bon Air Village was a place where a two-car garage was the exception. My mother and most of those nearby were stay-at-home moms. In Bon Air Village if you had a backyard fence at all, it was "sneaker friendly" and easy to climb over.

I wish to thank my wife Debbie for her patience with me as these books came to be. She assisted me beyond all of my expectations in the editing process, and she served as an essential, invaluable sounding board along the way.

Thank you to my sons Andrew and Jonathan for your encouragement to press ahead with these stories at each step of the development of the books.

And thank you, Robert, for putting the "burr under my saddle" before "The Bon Air Boys" ever saw the light of day.

I dedicate these books to my grandchildren, especially my firstborn grandson, Grant. My desire for him and them is that they grow up with wonderment and adventure in their hearts, seasoned with loyalty, honesty, love for God & country; respecting all adults *and* the down-and-out in life.

Greg Golden, Mobile, Alabama

About The Author

Greg Golden grew up in middle America, the youngest of three children and the only son of a pastor. Greg's love for literature was first demonstrated when at the age of ten he ran out of the forty-three Hardy Boys books available to read and he wrote one for himself.

After college, his career path took him to Mobile, Alabama where he met and married Debbie. There they raised two sons, and those sons and wives have given them numerous grandchildren, the newest loves and diversions in their lives.

Greg is an ordained minister and he frequently mentors those who come across his path seeking encouragement and guidance.

Contents

In several more seconds, the beam of a powerful flashlight appeared. It played on the back wall of the half-completed building as a figure holding it walked toward the structure. The moonlight barely revealed the form of someone, a large someone, entering an open door. Then, the source of the light beam vanished inside.

"Griff!" Frank whispered hoarsely at a volume loud enough to be heard across the graveyard. "Get over here! Something's not right. Somebody's just gone into the Rose Bowl, and it looks like they're up to no good!"

From "The Secret Of Hickory Hill"

The Secret Of Hickory Hill

GOOD DEEDS IN DARK PLACES

Chapter 1

"Wait up, you guys! It's not fair, just because you're taller than me," whined Frank Whidden. Frank took five steps to the others' four as he and his two friends made their way through one of the four-foot-wide concrete storm drains that criss-crossed beneath the streets of their neighborhood, Bon Air Village.

"Hey, at least you don't have to duck as far as I do," Chase Spencer retorted over his shoulder, as he sped up even faster.

"Be nice, fellas!" said Griff, the one who often assumed the role as peacemaker. "We've got the whole summer together, and you two just need to relax."

Frank and Griff had been friends and down-the-street neighbors for most of their lives. Chase moved into a house over the back fence and four doors down from Griff several years ago. The young teens' personalities were entirely different, but they got along well most of the time. Frank was three months older than Griff, but he was a few inches shorter. Griff took on the role of Frank's big brother and protector, so his efforts to smooth their verbal conflicts were regular, and he was called into action often.

"I see the opening!" shouted Chase, the leader of the expedition. His flashlight beam swayed back and forth with each step. There had been no rain for most of May and into June, so the storm drain was bone dry. Sand, dried leaves and twigs, as well as an occasional soda bottle littered the bottom of the concrete tunnel. The boys' sneakers crunched and slid on the debris as they walked.

Within a minute all three boys stepped out of the darkness of the storm drain opening and onto the grass of Snyder Park. As their eyes adjusted to the daylight, the only people in sight were two younger boys throwing a football back and forth a hundred yards away. Unseen birds chirped randomly from atop a nearby line of trees.

The air was still, and the late morning sunshine felt hotter and brighter than usual since the boys had just come from the cool and dark of the underground. It was the second week of June, within the first days of summer vacation in Lewisville, a town of 11,000 located along the New Haven River.

Frank led his friends toward the shade of trees that bordered the park. There, he dropped to the ground and slid back against a large elm. He stretched out his legs, interlocked the fingers of both hands, and placed them behind his head. Griff and Chase followed his lead. Nobody spoke for a full minute.

"What do you want to do now?" Frank asked his friends. "It's still about an hour until lunchtime."

"I don't care," Griff replied. "What do you want to do, Chase?"

"Hmmm... let me think." After a long pause, Chase blurted out. "We need a mission! We need something to do that will help somebody -- we need a project; a project like doing some good deeds, but in secret. If we can't think of something interesting soon, it's going to be a long, boring summer."

"Yeah! And we can do it unanimously so that nobody knows who did the good deeds!" Frank exclaimed.

"The word is *anonymously*," Griff corrected, "and I like your idea." He paused and then said, "How about we clean up the church graveyard? I noticed the mess in there yesterday. It's been neglected for years. I can get some yard bags from our garage, and all of us can bring rakes. I think my Dad has some hedge clippers."

"This'll be fun," chimed in Chase, "and there are some other places that I go past on my way to school that look like nobody has taken care of them in forever! We could start with the graveyard and secretly work our way to the river doing other projects. It'd be kind of like Robin Hood's gang, except we wouldn't be taking anything."

"Well I don't understand the last thing you said, but I like the idea," Griff said. "The tough part will be trying to keep it a secret. We'll have to be careful so people won't know who's doing the work. It'll be fun to keep everyone guessing!"

"All right," Frank said excitedly. "Tonight's the night! I'm going to see if my Mom can call your moms. You guys can stay over in our tent, and then we can leave together from my backyard. That'll make it easier to get started because we can head to the cemetery after everyone's asleep and put in a couple of hours' work. It'll be a lot cooler by then, too."

"Excuse me," Chase said, "but I was thinking this was going to be a thing we do in the daytime. It's a cemetery, for

Pete's sake. It's dark at night. I don't think I like this idea after all."

"Frank, it sounds to me like Chase is afraid of something that might be out there in the creepy nighttime in the graveyard. Is that what you heard?" Griff queried.

"That's what it sounded like to me...."

"All right, all right, fellas," Chase said, interrupting their taunts. "I'm in. Everybody bring your flashlight and your tools."

Chase suddenly stood up. "I just remembered that I have a list from school of books that I need to read during the summer break. The short ones are going to get checked out first at the library, so I need to make a trip there before they're all gone."

"Okay. We'll walk with you," Frank said, "and then I'm going to drop by my Dad's office to see if I can borrow some money for ice cream. I just heard the Dream Cream truck, and it's been a long time since breakfast. Let's go!"

The three headed toward the main street of Lewisville. Along the way, Chase split off from the group when they reached the City Library. At the next block, Frank and Griff parted ways. If everything worked out with their moms, the boys would all convene for a campout in Frank's yard later that evening.

....

By the time Frank had been home for only a half-hour, his mother had all the plans set up with Chase's and Griff's parents. The overnight campout had expanded to include a backyard cookout with Frank's mom and dad, his sister, and the three friends. There would be hot dogs, hamburgers, baked beans, chips, dip, sodas and big slices of watermelon to top off the meal. Frank's sister Kate wanted to add some cookies to the menu, and she got no argument from Frank about that.

Frank's dad owned his own insurance agency, so he had the freedom to come and go as he pleased. He left work early, and the two of them pulled their Army surplus tent out of the garage. They left it to air out on the back lawn as they searched for the poles and stakes. They were one stake short, but they found a croquet post to serve as a substitute. Frank's family camped regularly and had enough sleeping bags for their guests.

The afternoon flew by. At 6:00 sharp, and within a half-minute of each other, two bicycles -- one green 10-speed racer with low handlebars and one blue bike with high handlebars and a banana seat -- streaked onto the driveway of 318 Stafford Avenue. They each came to a stop in front of Frank's garage. Both boys had on a backpack which held their overnight clothes, toothbrushes, flashlights, and work gloves.

To carry out their first good deed mission as planned, each of the three, at different times in the middle of the afternoon, had secretly placed rakes, yard bags, and other tools along the back fence of the church cemetery.

"Welcome, fellas," said Frank's dad, greeting the two boys who he'd known for many years. As he always did, Mr. Whidden roughed up Chase's thick mop of hair and patted Griff heartily on his back.

"We're glad that you could come," said Frank's mom.

"Oh, we wouldn't have missed it for anything, Mrs. Whidden!" Chase exclaimed.

"Yeah," Griff added, "this is going to be the best summer yet, and it's starting here tonight!"

Frank and Chase shot a quick, anxious glance at each other, fearing their buddy was going to reveal their secret summer plans before they got underway.

"Well, grab a plate because the burgers and dogs are ready," Mr. Whidden announced.

As he spoke those words, Kate came through the back door with a tray of warm chocolate chip cookies. She was a pretty and pert girl, four years older than her brother Frank. She was known at the junior college to be a Dean's List student, the captain of the cheerleaders, and a formidable softball player. Many boys in her class wanted to call her their girlfriend. With shoulder-length brown hair, her crystal green eyes, and slightly turned up nose, Kate had little interest, for now, in her many admirers. She preferred to concentrate on her studies and doing volunteer work in the community.

After everyone paused and bowed their heads for a brief prayer of thanks for their meal, Frank's dad said, "Eat up, guys!" He only needed to say it once.

By 6:45 the table had been emptied of all food. Moans of satisfaction came from the three friends who had moved from the picnic table on the patio to the deck along the rear of the house. The trio sprawled across two Adirondack chairs and a recliner.

"Ugh!! I can't hold another bite. I might not ever leave this chair," Griff groaned.

"No wonder. You had two hamburgers, a hot dog, chips, two sodas, *and four cookies!*" Chase reported.

"Well apparently I'm still growing," retorted Griff.

"Growing wider around the middle," Frank sniped. They all laughed heartily at each other's misery and began to moan again.

By 8 o'clock the sky grew dark, and lightning bugs twinkled around the backyard. Everyone went indoors. The group played card games until Frank's parents excused themselves and headed to their bedroom. Within a few minutes, Kate covered a yawn and soon said goodnight to the three boys. Frank turned off the room lights except for one above the kitchen stove, and the friends made their way outdoors into the backyard.

....

It was just after 10 o'clock when they each claimed their places within the flashlight-lit tent. No one dared to actually lay down fearing that he might doze off and wake up to find his shoestrings tied together, his backpack tossed onto the garage roof, or worse. Consequently, whispered words about nothing of importance filled the next moments. When there came a lapse in their conversation, the distant chimes of the tower clock on the courthouse square broke through the quiet. Everyone listened in stillness until the eleventh gong sounded.

"Let's get it done, guys," Griff said.

Their plan was for the entire clean-up operation of the first night to be finished in two hours or less. If things went as planned, the boys would be back in the tent and sound asleep long before 2 o'clock.

Quietly, the friends stepped into the fresh air of the moonlit night. In single file they walked to the crossing streets of Third and Catherine. Turning right, the boys continued two blocks more under the canopy of oak and maple trees. No streetlights on that road aided their walk, so they stepped cautiously on the uneven sidewalk until they reached the Lewisville Community Church.

It was the oldest church building in town. The exterior was white, clapboard siding. There were elaborate stained glass windows on either side of the three hundred seat sanctuary. The main entrance was framed by peeling paint on raised trim that arched to a peak above the two wooden doors. Once active and full of life, nowadays on a typical Sunday scarcely forty people attended.

A stone's throw from the north side of the church was the cemetery, about an acre in size. A low fence of rusty iron with cracked, black paint formed its perimeter. Mature oak and maple trees towered overhead among the tombstones. Those trees cast dense shadows across much of the graveyard. The moonlight illuminated small patches of the ground here and there.

Most of the grave markers were modest, three-feet or less in height, but some monoliths rose prominently ten feet and more above the property. In daylight, a person could read the tombstone inscriptions, some of which dated the residents' burials as far back as the early 1800s.

The three friends went to work in silence. Frank and Chase raked leaves and pulled the vines and thistles that had encroached onto the graves and around fence posts. Griff snipped low-hanging branches with the clippers. Within the first ninety minutes they filled four large yard bags and dragged them to the gate entrance.

The town hall clock in the distance chimed the one-o'clock peal, and a few minutes later Frank and Chase reached the most distant fence line; the final part of the night's task. Beyond that fence were a drainage ditch and an empty field. Seventy-five yards further into the darkness, the Rose Bowl bowling alley was under construction.

Suddenly, the quietness of the night was broken by the unmistakable sound of a car door closing. Both boys localized the noise and turned their attention toward its source just in time to see the interior light of a vehicle start to dim and then go out. Their gaze froze, fixated on something that seemed very much out of place given the lateness of the hour. In several more seconds, the beam of a powerful flashlight appeared. It played on the back wall of the half-completed building as the figure holding it walked toward the structure. The moonlight barely revealed the form of someone, a large someone, entering an open door. Then, the source of the light beam vanished inside.

"Griff!" Frank whispered hoarsely at a volume loud enough to be heard across the graveyard. "Get over here! Something's not right. Somebody's just gone into the Rose Bowl, and it looks like they're up to no good!"

A TELLTALE TAILLIGHT

Chapter II

Almost instantly Griff sprinted from across the graveyard and stepped between Frank and Chase. With no sound other than crickets, the three stood breathlessly. Their eyes were fixed on the large, half-finished building.

Because of the moon's position, the rear of the Rose Bowl was partially in shadows. The vehicle parked there appeared to be a truck. It's roofline seemed too high to be a car. Although most of it was not visible, the moonlight revealed the front portion. As their eyes adjusted to the scene, they could see that it was light in color and it had chrome around the grill and headlights.

"What do you think is going on?" Griff whispered.

"I don't have a clue, but I think we should find out," Frank answered. "Let's get closer. We can duck into this drainage ditch and work our way over there without anyone seeing us."

The open, concrete ditch ran parallel to the rear fence of the cemetery. A short distance away it turned ninety degrees and followed the property lines of several homes on another street. By squat-crawling, they could get to within fifty feet of the intruder and remain unnoticed.

The three boys hurdled the iron fence, and then in another several feet they slid down into the ditch. The friends began their advance, uncertain if or when the stranger would step out of the building and back into the moonlight.

When they arrived at the best vantage point, they positioned themselves where they could now see that the truck was white, and it had a winch mounted on the front bumper. From that location they could also look directly beyond the truck and observe the door used by the intruder.

Their hearts were racing with nervousness and excitement, but they stayed totally still. Suddenly the beam of the flashlight appeared again in the doorway and swung toward them. Because of the tall grass between them and the building, the boys felt sure that the intruder hadn't noticed their presence.

As the man walked toward his truck, the three boys could see a large toolbox in one hand and a carton of some sort under the arm of his flashlight hand. He set them on the ground and lowered his tailgate. He placed those items onto the truck bed. The shadowy figure turned and once again walked toward the door, then disappeared into the darkness of the building.

Within another moment his flashlight beam cut through the night, and he approached the truck with his arms full of something long and cumbersome. He stowed it, and then quietly lifted and pushed the tailgate closed.

As he approached the driver's door, he stopped and seemed to survey the entire field. When the intruder turned his head and light in the direction of the boys, Chase instinctively ducked. As he did, his flashlight fell from his back pocket with a clang and a rattle as it rolled away from his reach.

"Come on, let's get out of here!" Griff whispered through clenched teeth.

As quickly and as quietly as they could, they duck-walked away from the Rose Bowl in the drainage ditch and headed toward the corner of the field. Chase stole a glance over his shoulder. The large stranger had walked toward their observation area, the place where they had been crouching. After a few seconds, he returned to his truck. The boys relaxed somewhat in the belief that he hadn't seen them or noticed their hurried departure.

They were out of breath, and their knees ached from their awkward retreat. The three stopped at the place behind the cemetery where they had entered the ditch. There, they turned once again to view the truck. Its headlights were on. The driver steered a half-circle in the unpaved area where he had parked. As he drove away, the three friends noticed that when he pressed his brake pedal, one tail light glowed red and the other glowed white. The truck was missing the left lens.

"I thought we were gonna' die," Chase said, expending more breath than sound. "That was way too close for me!"

"What just happened?" Frank asked. He didn't expect anyone to have a better answer than his thoughts.

Griff said, "People who are supposed to be in a place like that don't take things out of a construction zone at one o'clock in the morning; they don't use the back door; they don't use a flashlight; and they don't try to close their tailgate and door that quietly. *Guys! We just witnessed a robbery!*"

The sun was already high in the morning sky when the first of the friends raised on his elbows in the tent. The other two stirred restlessly. "What time do you think it is?" Frank asked.

After a few seconds and through a wide yawn Chase responded, "Nine o'clock, I'd bet."

"Knock, knock. Anybody alive in there?" The shadow on the tent and the voice from the backyard were Kate's. "Are you guys going to sleep all day?"

"We're getting up now," Griff replied. "We'll be out in a minute."

"Pancakes and sausage are stacking up inside, so you need to come while they're hot," said Kate as her voice trailed off toward the back door.

The three friends quickly made themselves presentable. No one spoke as they put on their shoes and straightened their bed-hair, filed into the pleasant kitchen, and dropped into their chairs. Tall glasses of orange juice were already by their placemats. A large platter containing pancakes, scrambled eggs, and country sausage patties invited the heartiest appetites to dig in.

Connie Whidden joined Kate in the kitchen just as the boys began to fill their plates. "Did you boys sleep all right?" she asked the group.

Chase darted a glance at Frank and then Griff as several seconds elapsed before anyone spoke. "That tent sleeps pretty well, Mrs. Whidden."

"Yeah," agreed Griff. "Thanks. We did."

"Your dad left earlier, Frank. He asked me to remind you that Mr. Rigsby's yard needs to be mowed. He said that there's plenty of gas in the can in the garage."

"I'll take care of it, Mom," Frank replied. "I thought Dad said he was going to work from his office at home this morning."

"He planned to, but something came up at his main office. Something about a police report and a break-in, and an insurance claim on some equipment of some sort."

Everybody froze. If Kate and her mother hadn't had their backs to the breakfast table, the boys' reactions would have given away their knowledge of that very situation.

"*Really?*" was all Frank could say, and he was immediately afraid that he had said too much.

"Yes. Some expensive things, as I understand it."

The friends sped up eating their meal so they might leave the table and get to a place where they could talk. In short order Frank, Chase, and Griff thanked Mrs. Whidden and Kate for breakfast and returned to the privacy of the tent.

"All right," Chase began, "we have a big problem. We know about that robbery, but I don't think we're ready to tell *what* we know, at least not yet."

"Yeah. Nobody told us *not* to be in the middle of the

spooky cemetery in the middle of the night, but I'm not sure they'd approve of it, either," said Frank.

"If we tell what we know, our clean-up projects could come to an end before we barely get started," Griff surmised. "Maybe we can do some snooping around and figure out who that guy in the pickup truck is. If we can come up with a name, we can get that information in the hands of the police – without giving away *our names*, of course."

"So do we agree? We'll act like we don't know anything – at least for a day or two – while we look for some clues. Is everybody in?" asked Chase.

With agreements around, the boys began to pack up their belongings and head for their homes for the day. They resigned themselves to be watchful for a white pickup truck with a winch, and to report anything unusual they might observe. They planned to speak again at 8 o'clock using the walkie-talkies that they each kept in their bedrooms.

"Remember to go back to the cemetery and get your tools sometime today, but don't let anyone see you when you get home with them," Frank said. With that, the friends said farewell. Frank went into his garage and prepared to help the elderly, family friend who lived nearby.

The Rigsby house was one of the oddities in the Bon Air Village neighborhood. Most of the homes were one-story, ranch-style homes, except for a few two-story houses here and there. Nearly all of them were built during the previous twenty years. The Rigsby place was three stories tall and had a broad porch with four white columns across the front. It was positioned so high above Goldstone Lane that passersby looked UP to the foundation of the large place.

Nobody else in the neighborhood had any idea how long the house had been there, but the rumors were that it dated back to the middle of the previous century. Leonard Rigsby, the current resident, was thought to be the last surviving family member of a long line of distinguished citizen Rigsbys.

Frank's grandfather had known this elderly neighbor for at least fifty years. Frank and his sister Kate had adopted him, now in his sunset years, as their Great Uncle Leonard.

Frank rolled his lawnmower to a stop on the sidewalk in front of the house. "Hi, there!" he said, waving to the gentleman who stood in the doorway of his home.

"Looks like we might have some rain by the time you finish," replied Mr. Rigsby. "I sure appreciate you coming over to help." His voice expressed kindness.

"Aw, that's no problem. I'll come ring the doorbell and visit with you before I go."

With a thumbs-up gesture, the frail Leonard Rigsby disappeared behind the tall, wood and glass door and pushed it shut.

An hour later, as Frank finished mowing the sprawling yard, Mr. Rigsby shuffled back onto the shaded front porch carrying a tray with two glasses of lemonade and a plate of cookies. "Come on up here and cool off, Frank," he said.

Frank wiped his face with his t-shirt, bounded up the steps, and sat down on the porch swing. He picked up two cookies and the iced drink as he did.

"How's your summer going so far?" inquired Mr. Rigsby.

"Good," was Frank's only reply. Then after a few seconds, he continued. "Mr. Rigsby, if someone you know saw something happen that was wrong, well, um, illegal, and that somebody didn't say anything about it, would that be wrong? I'm sorta' asking for a friend."

Leonard Rigsby's eyes widened a bit, and a faint smile crept across his face. "Well, that depends on whether your friend has all of the facts. If he doesn't know for sure what he saw, it would be more of a rumor than anything. And if he or she spoke about it without being 100 percent sure, it could hurt someone's reputation. How certain is your friend about what he thinks he saw?"

"Well, I believe he's fairly sure, but not 100 percent, and I know that he doesn't know *who* did it."

"Frank, I'd hope that your friend would get all of his facts together and perhaps tell his parents. They could help him report it to the authorities," Mr. Rigsby offered.

"That sounds like a good plan! Thanks for the cookies and lemonade! I'll see you sometime next week!" And with that said, Frank jumped up from his seat, skipped down every other stairstep, and began to push his lawnmower toward home.

The three friends needed proof, but first they needed more facts *and* hopefully the intruder's identity!

A Telltale Taillight   18

AN URGENT SEARCH

Chapter III

Chase switched on the power and listened to the hiss of static on his walkie-talkie speaker. He waited until his bedside alarm clock read exactly 8:00, then squeezed the transmit button and asked, "Hey guys, did either of you pick up my...?"

He stopped speaking in mid-sentence and released the walkie-talkie's button. Chase felt his face turn pale as he realized what the others hadn't known. After his flashlight fell from his pocket into the concrete ditch near the Rose Bowl, Frank and Griff led the way as they retreated. Scrambling to stay low and out of view, Chase followed them. In the darkness and in his hurry, he left his flashlight on the ground. Ordinarily, that wouldn't have been a problem, but a few months earlier with an electric etching tool, he had inscribed "C. Spencer" prominently along the barrel of it.

He pushed the transmit button again and said, "Guys, I don't know if it's a big deal or not, but my flashlight had my name on it, and I didn't pick it up when we were getting away. It looked to me like that guy might have gone to where I dropped it. That could be bad."

Griff spoke first. His voice crackled across the radio speaker with hopes to calm Chase's fears. "He might not have. It could still be there. I live the closest to the Rose Bowl. I'll wait until everyone's in bed, and I'll go check it out."

"*Not on your life!* You're not going there alone!" Chase

exclaimed indignantly. "It was *my* mistake. *I'll* go."

"We're in this together, buddy! We should all go," Frank said.

"All right," Griff continued, "can we meet up again tonight, say at 10:30? We can learn pretty quickly if it's still there."

....

The night air was sweet with the aroma of the honeysuckle blossoms that covered the fence outside of Frank's bedroom window. On mild summer evenings his parents preferred to cool their home with a window fan switched to exhaust mode. One whirred in an upstairs room bringing a fragrant breeze into their whole house.

His bedside alarm clock read 9:55.

Frank spoke into the microphone of his base station two-way radio. "It's thirty minutes until we agreed to meet. Are you guys still good for that?"

A hiss came from the speaker, and then Chase said, "Yep."

After a short pause, Griff spoke. "I can't find my sneakers."

Frank chuckled and smiled, then pressed the transmit button. "Remember that we're meeting at the corner of Wellington Avenue and Porter Road at 10:30. Don't be late. We'll head straight for the graveyard from there."

"Remember to wear dark clothes, guys," Chase added.

"See you two soon," Frank said, and then he turned off his base station.

....

Chase laid back on the lower bunk bed and propped himself against the pillows. He placed his crossed arms on his chest and exhaled. Down the hall from his second-floor bedroom, a majestic grandfather clock at least seven-feet tall ticked off the seconds as the pendulum swung left-right-left-right, over and over again.

Chase and his younger brother shared a bedroom, and Matthew finally turned off the reading lamp clipped to his headboard. In a few minutes, Matt was breathing heavily in the top bunk. It's a cinch he wouldn't awaken when Chase got up to leave.

He rehearsed in his mind which two of the stairs always creaked under his weight when he stepped on them. Chase hoped he wouldn't disturb anybody as he left.

Bong. The quarter-hour sounded from the clock and echoed through the house.

Griff stepped into the night air and stopped on his back porch. As he pulled the door closed, a neighbor's cat leaped off the porch with a yowl. Frightened by the unexpected presence of a teenage boy in that place at that moment, it disappeared into the shadows.

Frank was the first to arrive at the designated intersection. The June bugs that circled the streetlight overhead cast flickering shadows on the sidewalk around him. A block south a street-sweeper hummed as it slowly passed through an intersection. In a few more seconds it faded from sound and view. Other than that, the air was perfectly still.

A dark silhouette appeared fifty yards away and grew steadily larger. Someone's porch light illuminated the side of a familiar face. It was Chase. Then from a half-block behind him, the carefree stride of Griff appeared. Within a moment all three friends stood face-to-face.

Chase spoke. "This time let's cut along the side of the graveyard fence and go back to that same spot close to the Rose Bowl. We can walk in that cement ditch." He had given much thought concerning exactly where they were when his flashlight came out of his pocket. "Both of you guys have *your* flashlights, right?" Both Frank and Griff nodded affirmatively.

Dense cloud cover made this night much darker than the previous one. There was almost no moonlight present to help them with their search. As they approached the graveyard, they continued past the main gate and turned along the outside of the perimeter fence. The three of them ducked under low-hanging branches of the trees in the adjoining property.

When they reached the rear boundary of the cemetery, the boys sat on the ground and swung their legs over the edge and down into the three-sided cement drainage ditch. They turned and began walking to their left. Seventy-five yards ahead the drainage ditch turned to the right. At that corner was one of the openings into the underground maze of storm drains that formed the boys' stomping grounds.

Several apple cores were in the ditch where they made

the turn, and the boys crunched them underfoot as they passed by. "Those weren't there last night. I'm sure of it," Griff said.

In another fifty yards, they reached the place near the Rose Bowl where they had watched the intruder before Chase lost his flashlight. The three of them carefully searched the area covering a wide circle around that spot. They ran their hands through the high grass on both sides of the ditch. The only items they found were some empty soda bottles and a few damp newspaper pages, *but no flashlight.*

"That stinks!" muttered Chase.

"Yeah, but not so much because you lost a good flashlight. Somebody must have it, and that person knows your name, *and* they know you've been here," Griff explained.

"If they know about you, they probably know about us, too!" Frank added.

"Well, I'd say now we *really* need to stay alert and try to find the guy that broke into that building!" Chase said.

When Frank, Griff, and Chase felt they'd done all the searching they could do, the three turned and began to walk back toward the cemetery, retracing the same path through the ditch.

Suddenly, directly ahead of them a light flashed. It came from the opening into the underground storm drain pipe where it intersected with the ditch. The boys were less than a hundred feet from the glow. They immediately froze in their tracks and switched off their flashlights.

"Did you see that?" Griff whispered as he quickly crouched, wondering if his friends had seen the same thing.

The light became brighter as it played on the inside of the cement pipe and then emerged. Whoever held it swung it around the open field so that for a split second it pointed directly at them. After several more seconds, as quickly as he'd arrived, the stranger turned around, stooped over, and stepped back into the storm drain pipe.

....

TRACKING THE INTRUDER

Chapter IV

"This just gets stranger and stranger!" Frank whispered, shaken by what they had just seen.

"I'm going to have nightmares tonight," Griff said.

"Could you tell if that was the man from last night?" Frank asked of the other two.

"Not me. He's obviously not just a kid because he had to stoop to go back into the storm drain," Chase surmised.

As they hurried along, they talked while nervously glancing over their shoulders. All of the shadows on their route were now suspicious, and the whole idea of figuring this mystery out began to feel more dangerous than anyone had imagined.

When they reached their original meeting place, they stopped under the street light at Wellington and Porter. Frank told the others about his conversation with Leonard Rigsby from earlier in the day.

"I agree with him," said Griff. "I'd rather say nothing than tell a story that sounds like some kid's fairy tale. And we don't know for sure *what* was going on. It just looked really suspicious."

Frank spoke. "Well according to what my Mom said, somebody stole some pretty expensive things last night."

While they talked, from a block away, a vehicle turned

onto Wellington Avenue. It was headed toward where the boys stood. The approaching headlights seemed unusual to them, mostly because they hadn't seen or heard any other traffic during their walk to or from the cemetery. The vehicle slowed as it approached Porter Avenue and then it abruptly turned. While it was in the intersection under the beam of the streetlight, they realized that it was a pickup truck. And there was no doubt in anyone's mind that they'd seen it before. It not only had a winch on the front bumper; as it turned they saw its broken, left tail light!

All three boys looked wide-eyed at each other, then simultaneously took off in a sprint toward the safety of their neighborhood. In the last block before going separate ways, they slowed to a jog. With just a few words spoken, they agreed to meet after lunch in the park by the Frisbee field to talk through what they should do next. Nobody expected to get much sleep in the hours to come.

....

"Griffin, are you getting up soon? We have to be at church by 10. Did you forget that today is the meal distribution? It starts at 11." The voice from the bottom of the stairs was Mrs. Jenkins, Griff's mom. Barbara Jenkins was a homemaker and was everybody's Den Mother when they first became a Cub Scout. Her volunteer work around town was well-known and admired.

"Mom, I totally forgot. Can you do it without me this time?"

"I'm afraid not, son. I'm taking some pots of stew, and I know for a fact that a couple of our regulars won't be coming today. I need you to help serve. Remember, you didn't go last week."

Griff slowly became aware of the aroma of vegetable beef stew that reached his bedroom. His mom's request was reasonable, and he didn't mind helping. There would still be time to catch up with his friends after the meal program ended.

"All right, give me time for a quick shower, and I'll be right down."

Lewisville, like almost every town, had many families and individuals who were having a hard time paying their bills and providing good meals and adequate housing. Many residents of the town were out of work entirely. Several years ago Faith Family Church members launched a weekly meal program for anyone in need. It was more than a soup kitchen because, in addition to the hearty lunch for everyone that attended, they also gave each person a grocery bag containing dried beans, a box of powdered milk, two cans of various vegetables, a loaf of bread, and a small jar of peanut butter.

If an attendee stayed for the short preaching service at noon, they could then go into the second-hand clothing "store" and pick out two freshly washed and sized items. All of this was at no cost to those in attendance, and came from the generosity of the membership of Faith Family.

"What's the rest of your day look like?" Barbara Jenkins asked Griff as she drove them to church.

"Oh, Chase, Frank and I are meeting at the park at 1:00. We're just going to hang out a little bit. Nothing important. Just goofing off." After a moment he ended the silence with, "I've picked up the first book for my summer reading. I'm going to get all of them checked off my list soon."

"That's good to know, son. You'll be glad that you didn't procrastinate when it's time for us to vacation at the lake next month."

As they parked at the church, Griff and his mom joined several other volunteers already arriving. Some carried freshly pressed and folded trousers, shirts, blouses, and skirts into the church fellowship hall. Others, like the Jenkinses, brought with them food items including casseroles, loaves of bread, desserts, and containers of sweet tea.

The small group of early arrivers who assembled in several clusters away from the entrance at a corner of the building seemed uncomfortable to be there. People of all ages, shapes, and sizes were among them, and most dressed in ill-fitting clothing that didn't especially match the summer season.

A dozen volunteers inside the church worked quickly to get everything in position and ready. At 10:55 Pastor Bill Metcalfe called the full group to the center of the room. Around them were a dozen tables covered with white butcher paper tablecloths. On each table was a centerpiece -- a vase filled with colorful flowers donated by the town's florist.

"Let's gather here in a circle and hold hands while I pray," said the young preacher. "*We thank you, Lord, that you have provided us the opportunity to be helpers to those who are less fortunate than we are. Put smiles on our faces and let us show the love to others that you have so graciously shown to us. Amen."*

As people raised their bowed heads, Barbara Jenkins motioned to her son and whispered, "Go invite our guests to come in."

Griff opened the door and stepped into the sunlight. A crowd of at least fifty people had gathered in a line that meandered along the fellowship hall building and onto the sidewalk at its far end.

"It's ready, everybody. Come on in."

Griff was given the assignment of handing each guest a sturdy paper plate and a folded napkin that held a plastic fork, knife, and spoon. Some of the visitors looked at him as he gave them those items, but most kept their heads and gaze down. *It must be hard to accept charity,* Griff thought to himself.

He recognized a few of the guests from two months earlier when he had helped serve an Easter meal on Good Friday. That date fell within his school's spring break, so Griff and several of his buddies participated in that free lunch distribution.

At the end of the line, he noticed a tall, young man who had arrived several moments after everyone else. He was dressed better than most, but there was a rip in one elbow of his shirt. His black jeans were dusty, and his sneakers had dried mud on the edges of the soles. Griff guessed him to be 19 or 20 years old. When he handed him his plate and napkin, he noticed that the young man's hands were unwashed and his fingernails had grime under them.

"Welcome," Griff said with a pleasant smile.

"Thanks," said the guest who looked and smelled like he hadn't had clean clothes or a bath for many days.

"Take as much as you want," Griff told him. "You can have seconds if you'd like."

The young man moved slowly past the pans and bowls of food, piling roast beef, cornbread dressing, spaghetti casserole, green beans, and gelatin salad on his paper plate until it buckled in the center. He nearly spilled his food as he juggled the plate using both hands to support its weight.

With nobody else in line to be greeted or served, Griff left his post and caught up with the young man, who by then was serving himself a slice of pie and a brownie. "Let me get you some iced tea." Griff offered. "I can bring it to your seat."

"I appreciate that. That's very kind," was the soft response from the young guest.

....

The walk to Snyder Park was only four blocks to the east of the church. Griff could see his friends across the clearing before he arrived at the Frisbee area. When he reached them, he waited for a break in their conversation, and then said, "Fellas, I don't think I have ever been any more thankful for what all of us have than I am right now. I just came from seeing some really needy people. We are blessed, guys, I mean *very* blessed!"

"Oh, yeah. Today is the day for free food. So you helped serve, I guess?" Chase asked.

"Yeah, and it was tough realizing some of those little kids were getting the best and the most food of their week."

Frank chimed in, "While we were waiting for you, Chase and I've been talking about how we're going to get to the bottom of the robbery. I think if we could find the truck, we can just about wrap this case up and get back to our summer vacation and our clean-up projects."

"So," Chase said, "here's an idea. You know my cousin Donny? Well, he has a paper route, and it covers all of the streets on this side of the railroad track. If he'd let us ride with him this afternoon, we could hit every street and check every driveway for white trucks with bumper winches."

"Hmmm, I like it," said Griff as he rubbed his chin and looked into the horizon as if in deep thought. "Does he deliver papers in the morning, too, or just in the after-noon?"

"Both, I'm pretty sure," Chase said. "He drives to an end of each block, parks his car, then walks up one side of the street and back down on the other. Then he gets back into his car, drives to another street, and does the same thing. If anybody has a truck in their driveway, we'd see it for sure."

"I think we'd need to ask to go with him in the morning," Griff said thoughtfully, "because the afternoon paper always comes to our house by four o'clock, and most people aren't home from work until after 5. The morning paper usually comes before sun-up, so hopefully he'd let us ride with him early."

Frank spoke up. "We're all assuming that the guy lives on the good side of the tracks in Lewisville, has a regular job, and he parks his truck where you can see it from the street. It's a long shot, but I guess we've gotta' try something."

"All right, I'll check with Donny and see if he's okay with us going with him. Keep your walkie-talkies on after supper, and I'll let you know what he says," Chase said.

"Anyone want to take the underground shortcut back to the neighborhood?" asked Frank, the friend who was most often ready for spontaneous fun.

"Yeah, except we don't have our flashlights," Griff replied.

Frank reached into his front jeans pocket and pulled out a slim, penlight. He flashed it into the eyes of his two friends. "This should be good enough for our quick adventure. Let's do it!"

Frank, Griff, and Chase turned and crossed the Frisbee field toward the border of shade elms. They then descended the grassy incline to the large, drain pipe opening. Gray clouds had gathered since lunchtime, and because of that the air was noticeably cooler than earlier in the day.

It was a familiar place to the friends, and Frank entered the pipe first. He clicked on his pencil light to lead and light their way. They were back underground taking an often traveled shortcut home.

The Secret Of Hickory Hill

RISING WATERS

Chapter V

"No, Mrs. Morgan, Chase isn't home right now."

The caller on the telephone was from the Circulation Desk at the City Library.

"Yes, I'm sure he'll be glad that the book he wanted is now available. So, you'll hold it for him at the main desk? Thank you. Yes, I'll tell him. Goodbye, Mrs. Morgan."

As Chase's mom hung up the phone, the Spencer house shuddered from a blast of west wind. She looked through a window that faced the backyard just as their patio table fell over. A sun umbrella blew off their deck and tumbled across the lawn. A fierce storm with pelting rain and hail had not been forecast, but it dropped in suddenly over Lewisville, and it was delivering a downpour.

....

"You're stepping on my heel," Frank protested as the three navigated the storm drain. "Back off a little!"

The boys were a quarter-mile into their underground shortcut through the storm drainpipes and were headed toward their neighborhood.

Rainwater began to accumulate in the bottom of the cement tube. Chase and Griff could barely see the beam of Frank's penlight as they followed him. As familiar as they were with the maze under the neighborhood streets, the darkness lit by only a single, small light had become disorienting to them.

The route underground that should have taken five minutes had already taken ten. Where one drain pipe intersected another, they missed turning there and had to reverse their tracks. Doing so made Griff the new leader, so Frank passed his penlight to Chase, who gave it to Griff. That handoff to Griff didn't go well, and the small penlight fell into the flowing rainwater. Its beam went dark.

In the black and stillness of that moment, they stood frozen. For the first time, the boys could hear the distant echoes of thunder--and lots of it.

"Don't anybody panic," Frank urged. He hoped that his voice sounded more confident than he truly was. "The worst case is we can feel our way back to where we came into the pipe."

"I'd feel way better if we could have some light. Something hit my shoe after the penlight dropped," Chase said.

More echoes of thunder sounded around them. The rumbles came from the distant openings of the storm drains.

As he squatted down where he'd been standing, Chase put both hands on the bottom of the pipe and felt around in the flowing rainwater for the missing penlight. The stream was now four inches high and rising. "Help me search for the light, guys," he said.

All efforts were now focused on the recovery of the flashlight or its parts before the current of the water pushed those things out of reach.

"Hey, I got something!" Griff shouted. Then his enthusiasm vanished. "It's a battery."

"Oh, great! The light broke," Chase said.

"Let's keep looking. Maybe the bulb didn't break, and we can find the rest of it," was Frank's hopeful response.

All hands frantically searched the flowing water, which now was above the ankles of their shoes. The cement surfaces magnified the sound of the moving rainwater. The boys spoke loudly to be able to hear one another.

"I got the other battery!" Chase yelled.

Griff took a few steps in the direction the water was flowing and stuck his hands in the stream. He swept them back and forth and finally touched the smooth metal tube that once held the batteries and the bulb.

"I got the rest of it..." Griff said, and then he remembered that the cap to hold the batteries in place was the fourth and final piece. The cap, being the smallest and lightest, would easily have been caught by the moving water. It was probably long gone.

Griff backed up a few steps, joined the others, and reached into the darkness. He touched the arms of his friends. "Guys," Griff said, "I think we need to pray. We know we can get out of here by walking the direction the water is going, but we need to be safe down here, and it's getting worse by the minute."

The water had risen in just a few minutes to nearly knee deep, and the pressure of the flow made it difficult to stand.

"Yeah, let's pray, guys. I'll do it," Chase offered. *"God, you know where we are and what we need to do now to get out of here safely. Please help us trust you and not be afraid. Amen."*

....

The speed and amount of stormwater increased every moment, and as they trudged ahead the boys pressed their hands against the sides of the storm drain pipe to keep their balance.

As Griff led the friends, inch by inch, in total darkness, the sound and echo of the water and its turbulence around them changed noticeably. He recognized the difference as the intersection of another pipe joining the main one. Griff stopped and turned to Frank and Chase. "We're nearly home," he said.

As Griff continued toward the exit, he tripped over something in their path. The large but soft object was mostly underwater, and when he walked into it, he fell to his knees.

Chase, following on his heels, bumped into Griff as he stood up. Griff reached down to the obstacle in the water and he touched a strap. He quickly recognized it as a backpack – a completely waterlogged backpack! It had become lodged in the intersection of the pipes.

"I found something!" he exclaimed. "Chase, help me lift this thing!"

The two boys each held onto straps and they dragged it between them toward the exit of the pipe. Frank had to slow his pace to keep from overrunning his friends as they struggled to control the soggy pack. By this time no one had a square inch of dry clothing from his waist to his shoes.

Above ground, the weather was clearing as the fast-moving thunderstorm continued its track away from Lewisville. When the boys finally reached the opening of the storm drain, they were exhausted and drenched. The receding clouds that followed the line of storms brought a chill to the summer afternoon. The three shivered in their wet clothes.

Frank was the first to speak. "I always thought we were the only ones that go sewer-stomping. I guess not."

As soon as Chase emerged from the drainpipe, he began to inspect the backpack, working to unzip the compartments.

"What do you see?" Griff asked anxiously.

"Well, clothes mostly," Chase replied. "There's a book, some socks, and a pair of sneakers; here's a pocket knife."

Griff leaned over his shoulder for a better view. "Hey, those jeans and that shirt have paper labels pinned on them. It's like the way the ladies at church mark the clothes that we give away! They write sizes on them so the people will know which ones will fit! This backpack belongs to someone who has been to the meal and clothes day at church!"

"That helps a little with the mystery," Chase said, "but

what's this stuff doing in the stormwater drain pipes? *Who* stores their things down there?"

Frank joined in to unzip the last of several pouches. "Wait just a minute!" he said as he pulled a slender, shiny object from the final compartment. "It's your flashlight, Chase!" Holding it up he rotated it in his fingertips for the others to see. "There's your name, plain as day!"

....

The boys spent the next hour air-drying their clothes and shoes in the sunshine of Snyder Park. Each one speculated at length about what the different clues meant.

Up until this point, the only ones who were aware of the secret clean-up project, the robbery, the mysterious truck and its driver, and the waterlogged backpack were the three friends. They weren't sure that they could keep all of that to themselves much longer.

On the walk back to their neighborhood, they saw a familiar, shiny blue, two-door coupe parked at the end of Stafford Avenue. It belonged to Donny. Nobody within a hundred miles owned a car like that. The white tuck-and-roll interior was spotless. The outsides of both doors had been modified, and they had no handles. Exactly how a person got access to them was another mystery in itself, and the boys had never been able to watch closely enough to see what secret button or lever Donny pushed to spring open the driver's door.

"What's up, guys?" The voice was Donny's. He crossed the street and walked toward them from the last paper delivery of that block.

"It's good to see you, Donny," Chase said. "We were talking about you, and I was going to call you tonight. We sorta' have a favor to ask."

"What is it?" Donny asked while opening the trunk of his car.

As Chase began to explain, Donny continued re-filling his delivery bag with rolled and rubber band-bound newspapers.

"It's gonna' sound kinda' strange, and we can't really explain everything, but we're looking for a particular truck. We saw it in a place where it wasn't supposed to be, and the driver was doing something that looked suspicious."

Frank interrupted. "We're just trying to put together some evidence so we can tell what we saw to the police. If this guy lives in Lewisville, you probably pass his house twice a day on your paper route. We were wondering..."

Griff blurted out, "We wondered if we could ride with you maybe tomorrow morning when you do your route. The other night we saw a truck like the one that was at the robbery..."

Instantly Chase and Frank shot a disapproving glance toward their friend.

"Robbery!" Donny exclaimed. "What are you talking about? Where was this? What was stolen?"

"Well, it looked like a robbery," Frank said. "That's the part we need to be sure of before we go to the police. All we need is a way to find the truck with the broken tail light and a winch on the front bumper. We figured if we could ride with you we'd have the chance to see most of the driveways in this part of Lewisville."

"Look," Donny said, "I don't mind you three tagging along, but if it's tomorrow morning, you're going to have to be here early to help me get my stacks of papers rolled and banded. Be in front of the drugstore at 5 AM. We'll need to be on our way by 6 o'clock. It takes 90 minutes to make my route. Don't be late." He closed his trunk and walked to the driver's door. "You guys look terrible; like drowned rats! Where've you been?"

Just like every other time they'd been with him, Donny's door silently popped ajar a few inches untouched by any hand. He then pulled it fully open, slid onto the white vinyl driver's seat, revved the big engine to life, and was soon turning the next corner in the distance.

When his car was out of view, Griff turned to his friends and spoke philosophically. "I guess by breakfast tomorrow we can check at least *that* part of the search off our list. Maybe we'll find the guy."

....

A SUSPECT SURFACES

Chapter VI

Bleary-eyed and yawning, Frank, Griff, and Chase joined Donny in the amber light of the neon "CLOSED" sign of the Bon Air Drugstore. Before they arrived, Donny had already rolled and banded half of the morning edition newspapers for his route.

"There's a box of donuts on the front seat and some cartons of milk in a bag on the floorboard. Help yourself," Donny said, half-smiling but not looking in the direction of the boys. His hands were almost a blur as he made preparations to throw nearly 300 papers to homes in the eastern part of town.

"Thanks," the boys said in almost perfect unison.

"So, what do you think you saw with this robbery?" Donny asked. "I hadn't heard about anything being stolen around here."

Griff spoke up. "We started doing a secret, good-deed mission-project where we decided to clean-up some places in town and not tell anyone or take credit for it. Our first one was Tuesday night at the church graveyard."

"That was *you guys*? I heard some people at the gas station talking about that. That's pretty cool. I'm impressed. At night?? Tell me more."

As the four of them finished preparing the stacks of newspapers while consuming the dozen donuts, the three friends told him what had happened over the last days.

Donny paused for a moment as if to render a judgment, then said, "I don't know *what* you saw, but I'll admit, it seems suspicious. Let's load these in the trunk and get them delivered."

On the first four streets, the routine went as expected. Park. Walk the length of the block while throwing papers. Cross over to the other side of the road. Walk back to where the car was parked and throw papers along the way. Get in the car. Drive to the next block and repeat the same steps. On the fifth street, however, they were taken by surprise.

"*Look at that truck!*" Griff whispered hoarsely.

Backing out of the driveway two houses in front of them was a dusty, white pickup. In the early dawn light, they could see a winch on the front bumper. As the driver entered the street, came to a stop, and prepared to go forward, the broken tail light reflector glowed brightly in their faces. The four of them stopped in their steps. This truck was without a doubt the same one that had been at the Rose Bowl two nights earlier.

"Who lives there, Donny?" Griff asked as the truck drove away.

"I'm pretty sure it's.... um. I need to look at my receipt book first for when I collect payments for the papers each month. I can't say for sure. It's a fairly new account, but all of my information is at home. I can probably tell you that later today."

At the end of the paper route, Donny drove the friends back to their neighborhood. "If you want, meet me in front of the drugstore by 4 o'clock, and I'll tell you what I find out."

Once again, the passenger door popped open a few inches with no apparent help from their driver.

"How are you doing that?" Chase pleaded. After they all exited the coupe, Donny simply smiled and drove away, leaving behind a quick squeal from the wide, white-lettered rear tires.

"I don't know about you, but I can't wait until 4 o'clock," Chase said. "I'm supposed to get a book that's being held for me at the library. It opens at 10. Next door at the Court House are all the property records since this town was formed. I've been there a bunch of times with my Dad. I'll bet we can get the name of that guy easily. Anybody want to meet me at the library when they open, and then head to the courthouse to do some detective work?"

"I'm in!" Frank replied.

"I'll be there!" echoed Griff.

The three separated at the curb and returned to their homes.

. . . .

After showering, scrubbing newsprint ink from their hands, and eating breakfasts, each of the friends peddled his bicycle back to the center of town. They converged in almost perfect synchronization just as the clock in the tower above City Hall chimed ten times.

"We'll wait for you to get your book," Frank said to Chase.

Just after Chase entered the library building, a familiar face turned the corner and walked toward the two.

"Hi, Dad," said Frank. The insurance agency that Mr. Whidden owned was one block west of both the town square and City Hall.

"You were up awfully early this morning, Frank, and weren't you just at the house eating breakfast fifteen minutes ago when I spoke with your Mom on the phone?"

"Yes, sir. I was, but we came back uptown to do some research." With a nod toward the library, Frank continued. "When Chase comes out of there with his book, we're going to look up some stuff in the City Hall basement."

A puzzled expression came over Ralph Whidden's face, but before he could probe for details, Griff said, "Um, it's just to help us with a question we have about somebody's name that lives over on Meadow Drive."

"Well, if you need any help, or if Mrs. Banks isn't able to find what you're looking for, just call me, and I'll see what I can do."

....

The Property Records room was down broad, marble steps in the basement of the century-old Lewisville City Hall. As they entered the archives and records room, Mrs. Banks, her head still facing downward at her desk, raised her gaze over the tops of her reading glasses. She eyed the trio of unlikely researchers.

It was a cavernous room that contained row after row of shelves holding hundreds of binders with copies of deeds, land drawings, and building plans. Each one of them bore her color-coded system of identification.

"Are you boys lost?" asked Mrs. Banks.

"Oh, no ma'am," Griff replied confidently. "We need to find out who lives at this address?" As he spoke, Griff pulled from a jeans pocket a folded piece of notebook paper, and he placed it on the countertop.

"Need or want?" Mrs. Banks asked as she stood and walked toward the boys.

"B-both, really," replied Frank, fearing that this information might be harder to come by than they'd first thought.

"Hmmm. Let's see." Mrs. Banks pushed her glasses further up her nose and eyed the scrap of paper. She sniffed loudly; a sniff that seemed to say she didn't have time for such a trivial request. Suddenly she spun around and disappeared into the rows of shelves containing a century of Jeffers County property records. She click-clacked her heels on the marble floors until the boys couldn't hear anything but their own breathing.

Chase swallowed hard and looked at his two friends. No one said a word. A faulty fluorescent fixture blinked overhead. Almost as quickly as she vanished, Mrs. Banks returned carrying a large, burgundy binder. As she dropped it onto the counter and pried it open, dust came from the thick volume, and the smell of musty paper greeted their nostrils. She thumbed backward a dozen pages and then forward several more. Without turning around or taking her eyes off the binder, she reached behind her for a blank slip of paper and withdrew a yellow pencil lodged in the bun of her hair. With those items, Mrs. Banks hastily wrote down a name.

"There you are, boys. I hope that helps you," she said, handing the information to Griff, the closest of the three.

Outside again in the sunlight, the boys crowded together for the reveal of the name: *M. A. Hettinger*.

"Never heard of him," Frank said. "I'm not sure if this is going to help us at all."

"It's a start," Chase said. "At least it's a *piece* of the puzzle."

"Hey, wait a minute!" Griff exclaimed. "Isn't Hettinger the name of that farm south of town a few miles away down Highway 11?"

"You're right, Griff!" replied Frank. "We pass it all the time; old farmhouse sits back in the trees. It looks like nobody has lived there or done anything with it for as long as I can remember."

"Yeah, the barn leans, and it has one of those wind-powered propellors for pumping water up on a tower," Chase added.

"Let's go by my Dad's office," Frank said. "Maybe he knows if there's a connection between the two Hettingers."

The boys walked their bicycles a half-block, turned the corner, and continued another several storefronts to the insurance agency office Frank's dad owned.

When they pushed the door open, a chime alerted Mr. Whidden that the visitors had arrived. While the boys waited in the lobby, Mr. Whidden leaned partially into view through an open door down the hallway. His telephone receiver was pressed to his ear. With a smile toward his son and the friends, he held up one finger as if to say, '*I'll be with you in a minute.*'

For another moment they could hear his half of a muffled conversation dealing, apparently, with business matters. Then, he hung up the phone and stepped into the hallway, meeting them in the reception area.

Frank spoke first. "I think we have what we need, Dad. But do you know the name 'Hettinger'? Isn't there a Hettinger farm south of town?"

"Well, yes, or there *used* to be. A lot of people know it as Hickory Hill, but nobody's lived there since Lloyd Hettinger died more than twenty years ago. The estate was tied up with a family feud, and no one could do anything with it for all these years. But I'm curious why you're asking."

Chase looked at Griff. Griff looked at Frank. Then both Chase and Griff nodded their approval to Frank.

"We saw something, Dad. A few nights ago, after the guys stayed over in the tent and we cooked out, we saw something, and we've been trying to make sense of it."

"Okay. Tell me more," Mr. Whidden said, motioning for the three to be seated in the lobby. He retrieved a chair for himself from behind the empty receptionist's desk and rolled it toward them.

Chase spoke first. "Well, it was all my idea at first, but we decided not to waste our summer just loafing around. We wanted to do something to clean up a few places around town, but do it so that nobody saw us – so it could be a surprise...."

Griff picked up the explanation in mid-sentence. "And the church cemetery looked awful, so that was going to be our first project."

Mr. Whidden nodded with approval. "That's very mature of you three. I applaud your thinking."

Frank spoke up. "Well, while we were finishing up, we saw some headlights and a truck back by where they're building the bowling alley. It didn't seem right that it was there at the time."

Mr. Whidden leaned back slightly and then asked, "What time *was* it?"

"Close to one o'clock," Chase said. He suddenly felt deceptive and ashamed.

"I take it since there were headlights, you're talking about one o'clock *AM*, not PM. Am I right?"

"Yes sir," said Frank.

"Guys, I know that you're teenagers, but I'd like to know -- *your parents* would like to know if or when you plan to be out that late. I'm not very pleased right now with what

I'm hearing, Frank. I approve of what you want to do, but would you communicate better with me in the future?"

"Yes, sir. Sorry, Dad," Frank said on behalf of his buddies.

After a long pause that the three friends feared might lead to more chastisement or a restriction of privileges, Mr. Whidden leaned forward again and asked, "What do you think you saw that seemed out of place?"

Griff spoke up. "We moved up close to the truck by sort of crawling in the drainage ditch, and we could see somebody in the dark, loading boxes from inside the Rose Bowl."

Chase continued, "It didn't seem right. We saw the truck, and it had a winch on the front and a broken tail light, and then Frank said the next day that you went into your office early because some things were stolen overnight, and we put it together that we must have witnessed the robbery."

Without leaving space for anyone to insert a word, Frank continued. "And then the next day we saw that same truck over on Porter Avenue, and we thought we could help solve the mystery if we knew who it belonged to."

"Okay, whoa, whoa, time out! That robbery that your Mom mentioned wasn't at the Rose Bowl. I would have heard about that if something was stolen there. It was one of my clients over in Richfield who had some new tires taken from his tool shed before he had a chance to put them on his car. I don't know about the Rose Bowl guy at all, but that's not what I was dealing with that morning."

All three boys sank into their chairs and their shoulders dropped as they processed what they had just heard.

"Don't look so disappointed, boys. There's something else going on here because the phone call I was on when you came in was with an attorney for Miss Margaret Hettinger. He asked me about underwriting the liability of a clearing crew that's going to start working out on the Hickory Hill Farm."

Chase, Frank, and Griff sat taller as Mr. Whidden explained.

"There's been a rumor for a very long time that old Mr. Hettinger kept his money and valuables somewhere in his house or on his property. He didn't trust banks; didn't want anything to do with them after the Depression when most banks failed."

The boys looked at each other and began to stir with excitement. Mr. Whidden continued. "So Margaret Hettinger, his only surviving blood-relative, has finally gotten her claim to the estate through probate court, and she now has the deed. She has some ideas where he might have put his valuables, and she plans to begin the search for them in the next few days."

....

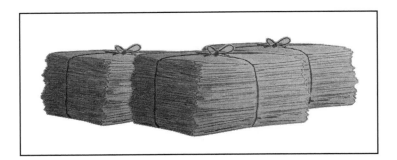

BIG DISCOVERY

Chapter VII

As the door closed to Whidden Insurance Agency and the boys mounted their bicycles, Griff was the first to speak. "I still don't get it. The truck at the Rose Bowl in the middle of the night doesn't make sense."

"There's probably a logical reason, but I'd like to know what it is," Frank said.

The return route to their neighborhood took them past the town square, and there along the curb was Donny's hot rod coupe with the trunk raised. Their college-aged friend had just come out of the hardware store carrying a bag of fertilizer. As the boys brought their bikes to a stop, Donny noticed them.

"Hey guys, I'm glad I ran into you. I was curious about that address, so I went home to check my records. Here's what I found. It's a her and not a him, and she's an older lady. I remember that now, and her name is Miss...."

"Margaret Hettinger," the three friends chimed in, interrupting in unison.

A puzzled look came over Donny's face.

"We couldn't wait for four o'clock, so we went to check the property records in the basement of City Hall," Frank explained.

"Well, I hope your curiosity is settled now," Donny said.

"Not mine," Griff said. "We still don't know who was driving the truck. Frank's dad said that the Rose Bowl people haven't reported anything stolen and that we misunderstood from his mom about the theft. It wasn't there, but it was in another town. So in my mind, there's still a mystery to be solved."

"Okay, I'll tell you what. When I'm collecting from Miss Hettinger as I walk my route this afternoon, I'll make some friendly conversation and ask her about the truck. One of you give me your phone number, and I'll call after supper and tell you if I learn anything juicy," Donny said as he closed his trunk.

"Write down my number, Donny," Chase said.

Donny walked to the driver door and, untouched, it popped open several inches. He opened it the rest of the way and reached inside for a pen and scrap of paper to make a note of Chase's telephone number.

"See you guys later," Donny said, and with a roar of twin glass-pack mufflers and a short squeal of tires spinning on the pavement, he was gone.

Frank shook his head and said, "One day I'm going to figure out how he does that door thing."

....

Just before 8:00 PM, the wall phone rang in the kitchen of the Spencer house. Chase got up from the desk in his bedroom and waited by the extension telephone in the upstairs hallway. He could hear his father inquiring who was calling, then he heard slightly louder, "Chase, you have a phone call. It's your cousin, Donny."

"Thanks, Dad," he replied in the direction of the downstairs as he picked up the phone receiver. "Hello."

"Chase, this is Donny. I think you're going to be interested in what I learned."

....

The walkie-talkie in Griff's and Frank's bedrooms crackled to life with the voice of Chase Spencer. "Hey, guys, are your radios turned on?"

Within a few seconds Frank replied, "Yep!" Several seconds later and sounding out-of-breath, Griff's voice came through. "You got me!"

Chase pushed the transmit button and began. "Here's what Donny learned. First of all, Miss Hettinger is the niece of old Mr. Lloyd Hettinger, the guy with the farm south of town. She's in her eighties, never got married, and like we already learned, as of a month ago she's the closest living relative, so she has been awarded the farm. You with me so far?" The radios all went silent momentarily.

"I am," said Griff.

"Me, too," said Frank.

Chase continued, "The guy with the truck, he's a great-nephew of hers, a college student from Taylor County, and he's staying with her while they go through the farmhouse and begin to clean it out. Nobody has done anything with it for like 15 or 20 years. And here's the answer to the mystery..." Chase paused for a more dramatic effect. "He's a civil engineering major over at State University, and what we saw at the Rose Bowl was him getting into town and picking up some surveying gear and the other things that go with it. His father is the project manager at that construction site, and he got permission to borrow them. Are you getting the picture?" Chase released the transmit button and waited for his friends to respond.

"This kinda' makes sense. What's the point of the surveying stuff?" asked Frank.

Chase continued "Well, Donny couldn't say for sure about that from Miss Hettinger. But remember what your dad said about the rumor about his valuables. When he died years ago, some of the family went through the house looking for it, but nothing turned up." Chase stopped speaking and listened for his friends to jump into the conversation.

Griff quickly asked the question that was now on all of their minds. "So the college guy and the surveying gear – are they thinking it's buried someplace, and they're going to dig for it?"

The speakers hissed for a moment. Not waiting for Chase to reply, Frank pressed the transmit button and spoke. "That equipment he borrowed might have nothing to do with the farm. We just don't know."

"Who wants to head out to a certain abandoned farmhouse Monday morning and take a look around?" asked Chase mischievously, already sure of the responses he'd hear.

"I'm in!" said Frank.

"Absolutely!" added Griff.

"Okay, we'll leave from my house at 9:00. Bring your radios."

. . . .

The New Haven River formed the northern boundary of Lewisville. To the south on Route 11, two miles from the city limits, a traveler entered rolling fields of wheat, tobacco, corn, as well as dairy and beef cattle. Family farms of 100 acres and larger were commonplace, and Hickory Hill, the Hettinger farm, was one of the biggest spreads, spanning 325 acres.

Thirty years earlier a dozen people lived on the grounds and tended the duties of a highly successful enterprise. After Mr. Hettinger's death, no one had the legal authority to carry on the operations. Within eighteen months the known cash reserves were gone, and the machinery, cattle, and vehicles were ordered to be sold by the courts. The earnings were placed in a trust for whoever the heir might eventually be.

A widower with no living children, Lloyd Hettinger died suddenly and hadn't filed a will or any instructions with his attorney or the courts regarding the distribution of his estate. Property taxes had been deducted from the trust by the county until all of the known money was gone. The utility company turned off the electricity nearly two decades ago.

The main house had once been an impressive white

clapboard-over-logs structure with elaborate millwork, moldings, and spandrel. With its wrap-around porches, the residence had the look of a gingerbread house. After more than twenty years of weathering and neglect, it was a shadow of its former glory. Trees and overgrowth hid most of the house from the view of passersby.

At a quarter past nine on Monday morning Griff, Chase, and Frank turned their bicycles off Highway 11 onto a driveway that was barely distinguishable from the dirt and weeds that had overtaken it.

"Gosh, it must have been a great place to visit back in the day," Griff said as they carefully maneuvered along the gravel path a hundred yards from the highway.

"I wonder if they're going to tear it down now," Frank said wistfully.

"Let's see if we can get inside," Chase said as they laid their bikes down under the shade of hickory trees in front of the house.

The white picket fence that once framed the yard was mostly rotten wood, and only parts of it were still standing. The gate lay on the ground.

As the three approached the front porch, they were surprised to realize it was bigger up close than it seemed to be from the highway. The scale of the doors, windows, porches, and roof height was much greater than they expected for a farmhouse.

The steps that led from the yard to the entrance were stone and mortar, but many of the boards that made up the porch, once painted dark green, were rotting or missing altogether. A chain attached to half of a rusting light fixture swung overhead in the breeze.

When they reached the front door, cobwebs and the leaves from many autumns blocked their way. The three boys carefully removed the debris, evidence that no one had walked through the door in a very long time.

To their surprise, the porcelain knob turned easily, and the ornate, glass and wood door pushed inward. Chase, Griff, and Frank looked at each other wide-eyed, and their astonished expressions silently asked the question, "*Who wants to go first?*"

Without hesitating, Chase stepped into the foyer. "I guess they would have locked it if they didn't want anyone in here."

A dozen feet inside the open door the three friends stopped and stood to look in different directions. In its day, this would have been the most spectacular home in Jeffers County. The ornate, two-story foyer was their vantage point to see a curved, dark oak staircase, brass wall sconces, framed oil paintings, bookshelves, carved paneled walls, and the heart of pine plank floor. Everything in sight was coated with a haze of gray dust.

"What are we looking for anyway?" Griff asked his two friends. "People have already searched high and low for Mr. Hettinger's will and valuables. What chance do we have of finding anything important?"

"We have..." Frank said, trying to sound dramatic, "fresh eyes!" As everyone laughed, Griff playfully punched his friend in the arm.

"Well, you better put your fresh eyes to good use because we don't know how long before someone comes along and runs us out of here," Chase said. "Be on the lookout for anything that seems wrong or seems out-of-place; a drawer that won't close or a wall panel that doesn't lay flat. You guys brought your flashlights I hope." The others nodded yes. "Okay, let's head to the top floor and work our way down. Holler if you see something suspicious."

The curved staircase was wide enough for three boys to ascend side-by-side. At the second floor landing, there was much less daylight. They continued and walked up another set of narrower stairs that led to the third floor. There they found three small rooms on each side of the hall. All of the rooms had ceilings that sloped corresponding to the roofline of the farmhouse.

The ones on the top level were furnished the same, each with a modest, single bed, and a nightstand with a lamp. They guessed that these rooms might have once been occupied by maids or housekeepers; perhaps a cook or a butler.

A bureau with four drawers was positioned facing each bed. Simple mirrors hung in all rooms next to the doors. A closet was adjacent to each bed. Most of the wallpaper in these rooms had peeled and come loose. All of it had faded during the many years the house had been abandoned.

One by one the boys inspected the rooms, and they looked especially closely in the closets and the bureau drawers. It was evident that many years earlier someone had searched the spaces because the nightstands were moved, drawers stood partially opened, and closet doors were ajar to different degrees. After each boy had investigated two rooms apiece, the three of them returned to the hallway.

"Nothing unusual in my rooms," Frank said.

"Me, neither," reported Chase.

"Do you suppose anybody's even been up here in the last twenty years?" Griff inquired. "I left shoe prints in the dust. You could go back and see exactly where I stepped."

As they descended the steps to the second level, they all felt that this area would be more promising. There were fewer and much larger rooms, each furnished with heavily carved and stained beds, and sitting areas with upholstered chairs. All of the walls, including the hallway, had mahogany wainscot panels; panels that were as tall as the teens.

Frank offered the instructions this time. "Okay, let's be extra observant here. We may only get this one chance to search. I guess some people think Mr. Hettinger buried his valuables outdoors since they couldn't find anything in the house. I don't believe I'd want to be that far away from whatever I was keeping hidden, especially if I didn't trust people or banks. I'd want my valuables in sight or at least close by."

"We should stay together for now. The three of us can check out a room faster if we do it all together," Chase offered. Nobody argued with his reasoning.

On the far wall of the first room that they entered, a large, faded, State University pennant caught their eyes. Across the top of a bookcase were many trophies for various high school and college sports achievements. On other shelves, the dusty spines of books had titles that suggested a boy once called this room his. A stuffed deer head and a mounted large-mouth bass flanked either side of one window, and those items further confirmed their thoughts about the occupant being a Hettinger son.

"Tap around on the wall panels, guys," Griff said. "See if any of them sound different from the others."

For the next several minutes no one spoke as everyone rap-tap-tapped high and low on the wainscot panels, hoping for a clue to a hidden door leading to a secret storage bin. The room yielded no such discovery, so they all moved across the hall to the second bedroom, the most elaborately furnished of the four rooms.

"This must be the master bedroom," Frank said. "The headboard is twice as tall as the one in the first room."

"Yeah, look at that huge cabinet for hang-up clothes," said a very impressed Griff.

"It's called a chifferobe, Griff," said Chase. "It's the same thing that Peter and his friends crawled into in the book "The Lion, The Witch, And The Wardrobe.""

"Wow, I could live inside of that, it's so big!" Frank added.

After every drawer was opened and closed and every foot of the walls around the room was inspected and tapped on, the boys concluded that nothing in there was exceptional.

While leaving the room, Chase took one final look over his shoulder and then suddenly stopped. "Guys, wait! Look," he said excitedly. "Look at that painting next to the window. I missed seeing that."

Within a modest wooden frame was the oil painting of a hillside scene. The pigments had no doubt once been vivid and beautiful. After so many years they had aged, turned dull, and were dust-covered. Added by the artist over the image of the landscape were the handwritten words of a Bible verse, Matthew 6:21: "Wherever your treasure is, there will your heart be also."

"What do you make of that?" Frank asked.

"I think it could be important," replied Chase. "This must be Mr. Hettinger's bedroom! It obviously meant something to him."

"Maybe," Griff added, "but what do we do about it? Where do we look next?"

....

THREE PLUS TWO

Chapter VIII

"Let's keep looking. That makes two of the big rooms inspected on this floor and two more to go," said Chase. "You guys check out the one on the left, and I'll take the one on the right. I'll meet you back here in the hallway."

"And then we can go downstairs and tackle the main floor," added Griff.

Frank and Griff crossed the hall and entered the room that shared a wall with the boy's bedroom. Chase went into the one that shared a wall with the master bedroom.

After scarcely five minutes Chase strolled into the bedroom Griff and Frank were searching. "Are you guys getting close in here?"

Griff turned toward Chase with a look of surprise. "We're making progress. What's your hurry? You didn't finish already, did you?"

"No hurry," quipped Chase. "and, yes. I checked everything in my room; the furniture and the walls, but apparently I'm faster than you guys."

Frank bore a puzzled expression. He left the room he and Griff had been inspecting and crossed the hall. In a moment he returned scratching his head and said, "Take a good look around this room guys, and then follow me across the hall."

Frank led Griff and Chase into the bedroom Chase had

just inspected, and looking methodically in each of four directions he said, "Something's not right, fellas. The first and second rooms -- the boy's room and the master bedroom -- are across from each other, and they're the same size but with different furniture, right?"

Griff and Chase agreed with a nod.

"These last two are directly across the hall, but one seems smaller. Look at this, Chase," said Frank as he pointed to the wall that was shared with the master bedroom. "This space is at least three, maybe four feet shorter than where Griff and I were. That's why you finished before us. There is less area and less furniture here!"

They returned to the hall and moved between the two rooms. Each boy observed the layouts of the spaces and came to the same conclusion: one was definitely smaller.

Suddenly the squeal and the loud pop of air brakes cut through the stillness of the second-floor hallway. A diesel engine outside rattled to a stop. The sounds came from the rear of the house. The three friends rushed to the nearest window to see two men walking to the back of a long, yellow trailer. On it was a tractor with a bush hog attachment, and as the boys watched, the men began to release the tie-down chains from either side of their load.

"We need to go!" said Chase with an urgent whisper.

In less than a minute the friends exited the farmhouse, pulled the door closed, and crouched in the tall grass by their bicycles. The unloading of the tractor and bush hog was underway directly behind the house, so they believed the two men hadn't seen their bikes in the front yard.

They felt that they stood a better chance of staying unnoticed if they walked their bikes back to the main road as they departed.

Because the farm area was in the highlands, and Lewisville was in a river valley, they coasted more than peddled during the two miles back to town. Their adrenaline was surging following the discovery on the second floor of the Hettinger farmhouse. The fact that the bush-hog delivery men almost discovered them added to the boys being out of breath as they rolled back into town. They finally eased their pace and spoke.

"My mind won't slow down thinking about what might be behind that wall between those bedrooms," said Griff. "I'll bet that a lot of old houses had hidden rooms and secret staircases."

"Yes," agreed Chase, "and we gotta' get back in there before all kinds of people show up when the clearing starts."

"Maybe my Dad knows their work plan since he is handling their insurance now. I'll try to find out from him without explaining why," Frank said.

The three neared their neighborhood and Mr. Rigsby's house came into view. The elderly gentleman was seated on his front porch swing reading the newspaper. As he peered over his wire-rim eyeglasses, he caught a view of them and he waved his hand, motioning for them to stop by.

"Hi, Mr. Rigsby," said Frank. "It's good to see you again."

"I'm happy to see you, too, Frank."

The boys laid their bikes down on the front yard and climbed the steps to the house.

"Do you remember my buddies Griff and Chase?" Frank asked.

"Oh, yes. I'm glad to see you, boys. Won't you visit for a few minutes? I made a pitcher of lemonade a little while ago, and I'd be happy to share it with you."

"Sure!" was their reply. It was nearly noon, and the sun felt unusually hot now that they were no longer aboard their bikes with the wind in their faces. His invitation brought them welcome relief.

As Mr. Rigsby entered the house and the door swung closed behind him, the boys pulled three wicker chairs into position near the porch swing and sat down.

In a moment he returned. "I hope that you won't mind a few cookies with your lemonade," he said with a wink and a smile. "They're not homemade, but they come highly recommended by the clerk at the market."

"This all looks great," said Griff. "Mr. Rigsby, I'm pretty sure you know my grandparents from church, Ray and Jewel Jenkins?"

"I sure do! Wonderful people, just wonderful."

"Mr. Rigsby, you know the Bible pretty well, don't you?" asked Frank.

"Well, I guess I do. I can always dedicate more time reading it each day, but it's my favorite book. I look to it for wisdom. There are truths in the Bible that will surely set our lives in the right direction if we will follow them. Do you have a question about something in it, Frank?"

Chase, unable to wait for his friend to form the question for their host, blurted out. "There is a verse we heard about that talks about a treasure and a heart. Does that mean like a buried treasure of gold or something like it?"

Mr. Rigsby slowed and stopped the motion of his porch swing, sipped again from his lemonade glass, and leaned forward. "Now that's a question many people have. I believe you're referring to Matthew chapter 6. Jesus was teaching his disciples, and a crowd began to follow him, so he and his twelve stopped. They all sat down to listen to Jesus. It is the longest single message in the Bible, and it extends across several chapters."

Mr. Rigsby continued. "His point to them and the many who had gathered to hear him was that whatever we value the most will be what we seek after. Jesus was alerting, actually *warning* them to be sure that they place the highest worth on and pursue things that have eternal value. You see, boys, anything here on earth in this life that we can gather and store will eventually rust or fail. But the things that will truly have lasting benefit are serving others, prayer, and obeying God. So Jesus was including money and possessions in his teaching, but it was about more than just *things* -- it was also about our attitudes and priorities."

There was a pause while the three friends thought on the wisdom of Mr. Rigsby. Breaking the quiet of the moment, the front door opened suddenly, and a tall, young man appeared. His arms were precariously wrapped around a dozen large three-foot long cardboard tubes. The young man seemed startled to see the guests, but then he spoke. "Oh, I didn't know you had company. I'm sorry to interrupt, Mr. Rigsby."

"That's quite all right, Thomas. It's perfectly fine," said their host. "Boys, meet Thomas Wilson. He's helping me clean up and organize things in my basement. It seems I'm prone to hold onto more than I move along. Reverend Metcalfe connected me with Thomas, and he has been a great asset to me during the past few days."

Chase and Frank were seated across from the door within view of the young man, and they nodded to Thomas as Mr. Rigsby spoke his introduction. Griff's back was to the door, and he turned in his chair to make eye contact with Thomas. When he did, Griff immediately stood. *"You're the, you're... I met you on Thursday when we served the meal at church!"*

It was the quiet young man with the dirty fingernails; the last guest who had come for lunch at the church that day. Thomas nodded to Griff.

"So you've met already?" Mr. Rigsby said. "Thomas hasn't been in Lewisville very long, and I'm employing him for now until he can get on his feet again. He is an excellent organizer, and Reverend Metcalfe knew that I wanted to get this old house in order. He started helping me here on Friday."

Thomas addressed the boys to explain. "My family is from upstate, and as of last year there was only my Mom and me, and then she got sick, and we lost our house."

Mr. Rigsby added, "Thomas' mom passed away a month ago, and he came to Lewisville a couple of weeks ago looking to start a new life for himself. It hadn't gone very well for him until just recently. I have extra room. He needs a place to stay, and I can certainly use his help."

Thomas appeared grateful to have a purpose and a place to belong. "The reason I came upstairs was to ask about these tubes, Mr. Rigsby. There are probably a hundred of them or more. Do you want to keep these, or should I put them in the pile for the landfill?"

"Oh, goodness. My drawings. I hate to part with them, but...."

Griff interrupted his train of thought. "You're an artist, Mr. Rigsby?"

"Oh, no, son. Not an artist like you're probably thinking. Not at all. These are drawings used for construction – blueprints, actually. You see, in my working days I was an architect, and during my career, I was able to design many of the buildings and the larger homes in this part of the state. Very often I kept a set of building plans for myself. It seems as if that practice has finally caught up with me."

Mr. Rigsby turned to Thomas and addressed his question. "I guess you should take them out back to be hauled away."

As Thomas juggled the many cardboard tubes, Griff helped him with the door as the young man backed into the house. "It was good to meet you all," he said to the three guests as he retreated, and then he was gone from view.

Frank was unable to contain his curiosity and burst out with the question the other friends were thinking. "Did you design the Hickory Hill farmhouse?"

"I'm old, but I'm not that old," said Mr. Rigsby, his eyes sparkling with laughter. "That house was there when I was born, and I guess it had been there for at least fifty years when I was earning my architecture degree at the university. It was one of the houses we studied in my classes. It's was a spectacular example of Classic Victorian; a beautiful structure in its day."

"So do you remember anything about it? Have you been in it before?" Griff asked hopefully.

"It has been many years, but, yes, I have visited it before. I recall knowing that one of the porches was added after it was built. The kitchen was enlarged around the same time."

"Mr. Rigsby, what about a secret room?" Chase asked. "Do you think that's possible there? Do you remember anything like that when you studied it, because we saw something on the second floor that didn't seem quite right to us?" The other boys were surprised that Chase revealed their exploration so quickly, but they could scarcely wait to hear the response.

"Now, that I can't say for certain, but it's possible. Secret rooms and safe rooms have been incorporated into construction since the Egyptians built the pyramids. There's an old hotel over in Campbell County with a guest room that many years ago was always reserved by a certain gangster when he stayed there. The room had a secret door inside a closet. It led to a passageway to help him escape if the police came for him. Since I know some of the history of that farmhouse, a hidden room in there wouldn't surprise me. But you say you've been to Hickory Hill? When was that?"

Frank spoke up. "We actually just came from there. You see, my Dad is helping with the insurance that Miss Hettinger needs for whenever they start working on the house and land."

Mr. Rigsby rared back on the swing, lifted his head, and let out a hearty laugh. "So Margaret finally prevailed and won the estate. Oh, that's great to hear! She is so deserving of it after the long fight among the family."

The three looked at each other and broke out in broad smiles. The boys were relieved that their secret was actually out in the open. Maybe there was an advocate in Mr. Rigsby after all.

"Boys, I think we should take a little road trip and do some deeper investigating into this discrepancy you noticed. I don't drive any longer, but Thomas has already taken me to the market in my sedan. I'll get him redirected away from his organizing to join us in our expedition. The three of you bring your bicycles up on the porch, and he and I will pick you up down the driveway at the curb. We're going exploring!"

....

DIGGING DEEPER

Chapter IX

Mr. Rigsby's spacious car seemed to float, more than roll as they drove toward the farmhouse. It shrugged off all of the bumps and turns through Lewisville and along the two-miles further south on Highway 11. Thomas wasn't familiar with the route, so he listened and nodded dutifully to all of the reminders by Mr. Rigsby; stop here; drive slower, and turn there.

In only moments the aged, dark green sedan was parked next to the front yard gate of the Hettinger house. As they arrived, the boys noticed that the tractor and bush hog were in the same place as earlier, but the truck and trailer that delivered them were gone.

Mr. Rigsby shook his head as his eyes scanned the farmhouse. "It is a shame how much the place has deteriorated over the years. I hope that Margaret has plans for returning the house to its original grandeur."

As he opened his passenger door, he turned to the three friends and said, "Come on. Let's take a look. You, too, Thomas."

At his advanced age, Mr. Rigsby was slow and cautious as he crossed the yard. The porch steps were an even greater challenge, but within several minutes they were all inside the house at the base of the staircase. "Thomas, would you help me with these steps? You three boys go ahead. We'll be along shortly."

Frank, Griff, and Chase bounded up the curved staircase hoping that this trip would answer more questions than the previous one. Griff realized as they reached the next level, that in their haste to leave earlier, he had left his shoulder bag behind. It was draped over the banister railing on the second floor. He retrieved the bag and placed one arm through a strap. Then, out of respect for Mr. Rigsby, they waited for him and Thomas to ascend the steps before they went further into the rooms.

Mr. Rigsby shuffled into the first and second bedrooms. He spoke admiringly of the structure and furnishings, and commented on how solid the old farmhouse still seemed.

Reaching the third room, Frank said, "This is the room that got us to wondering what was going on up here. See how the others are the same size, but this one is smaller?"

Mr. Rigsby pulled a retractable tape measure from his trousers pocket and stepped into the corner of the bedroom in question. He tugged on Griff's arm as he passed him. "Come with me, son, and stand over there," he said, pointing to a corner. "Now hold this end tightly against that wall, and I'll stretch it out to the other side."

Leonard Rigsby noted the reading on the tape measure and ambled out the door without any words of warning. That motion nearly caused the end of the tape that Griff held to pull out of his grip. Amid the chuckles of the two friends and Thomas, he managed to hold onto it, and he quickly caught up with Mr. Rigsby.

The gentleman entered the room directly across the hall with his measuring tape still outstretched and clacking against the doorway and on the floor. Mr. Rigsby let out an, "Oh! Oh, I see what you're saying. These room sizes don't seem to be the same at all!"

In the larger room, Griff went into a corner holding one end of the measuring tape. Mr. Rigsby stretched out his tape, noting the length he had measured in the prior room and compared it to the new measurement.

"Oh, my," Leonard Rigsby exclaimed, "we're fully four feet longer along this wall. But let's check a third room before we make any final assumptions."

As the three friends and Thomas followed closely behind, Mr. Rigsby entered the first bedroom, the Hettinger boy's room. Extending the tape measure with Griff's help, the conclusion was the same. The bedroom that adjoined the Master Bedroom was smaller, and it seemed to be that way for a reason.

"Okay, let's look for an access point into this void, the space between these bedroom walls," their elderly friend said. "Chase and Griff, you start with the closet in the smaller room and feel along the walls. Tap carefully and listen for a change of the resonant sound of the panels. Frank, you and Thomas come with me to the master bedroom, and we'll do the same along the wall that these rooms share."

For the next ten minutes very little was spoken, and each person pushed on panels, pulled on pieces of wood molding, tapped on walls, and listened. Their efforts yielded nothing.

Frank went into the master closet and pushed on the wainscot panels inside of it. He tapped, listened, and tugged on the trim and the coat hooks that lined the wall just inside and to the left of the door. One of the pegs appeared loose, and as he wiggled it, the peg flipped upward. From inside that wall he heard a scraping sound of wood-on-wood. Instantly, from the bedroom, Mr. Rigsby's shrill voice exclaimed, "That's it! We found it!"

Frank quickly stepped out of the closet and into the bedroom to see a jubilant, elderly man, a confused Thomas, and Griff and Chase dashing over from the room next door. There, just next to the chifferobe was a gaping, two foot wide opening where a wainscot panel had slid aside. A draft of stale air from within the dark gap flowed into the master bedroom.

"Who has a flashlight?" Mr. Rigsby asked. "Oh, this is exciting!"

Griff produced his penlight from a jeans pocket and handed it to Mr. Rigsby. "Be careful, sir," he cautioned.

Frank switched his small flashlight on as well and shined it into the opening. Mr. Rigsby ducked slightly, stepped over the baseboard, and entered the hidden room. He stopped, evaluated his surroundings, and after a moment looked back toward the boys.

"There are steps in here that lead down a short way and appear to turn. I'm going to follow them," said Mr. Rigsby.

One-by-one, each of the remaining four stepped over the threshold and ducked into the darkness. Frank was the last to enter, and he shined his light to benefit himself and Thomas.

Within the three feet of space from wall-to-wall, each step

was about eighteen inches wide. Dividing the two flights of the steps was a handrail to help a person navigate the stairs. At the next landing, the steps turned in the opposite direction and descended still further into more darkness.

"Are you fellows okay back up there?" Mr. Rigsby asked. "I've reached another landing, and we're still going down. Are you with me?"

"Yes." "Yes, sir." "We are," the others replied.

Their shoes treading on old, dusty wood were the only sounds until finally, Mr. Rigsby hollered over his shoulder. "I'm at the bottom and there's a door. It's unlocked, and I'm going in!"

The expectation among them was intense. Each person had already imagined what might be at the end of the hidden staircase: gold bars, a chest of cash; possibly rare gems. They were about to find out together whatever there might be.

As Frank and Thomas caught up to Chase and Griff, Mr. Rigsby had already been investigating the eight-foot by eight-foot room. The walls were of large, rectangular stones. Wooden shelves lined two of the walls. A small desk and chair were placed against a third wall. On the shelves, they could see a supply of candles, a tinder box with flint, and a jar of sulfur-tipped matches. Another shelf held three wooden boxes and several small, oak casks. At the top of the fourth wall was an opening one brick in height by three blocks in length. It was the apparent source of ventilation. A sliver of light came through that gap.

"By my estimates, we are at the level of the cellar. The only way in or out seems to be by the steps we just came down," Mr. Rigsby said, standing with his back to the desk. "Is everyone still okay?" Each of the four acknowledged that they were fine.

"I want you to see something. I think this may answer some of the questions that have plagued this family for over twenty years." After he spoke those words, he stepped aside and turned the penlight on an open Bible atop the desk. The two pages visible displayed chapter 6 of Matthew. Placed as a bookmark in the Bible were several folded pages of yellowed parchment paper. Written on the top sheet with large and swirling pen strokes were the words, *"The Last Will And Testament Of Lloyd Hettinger."*

Slowly and deliberately Mr. Rigsby announced, "Men, I think this mystery and the feud within this family can be wrapped up right here in this special and sacred room."

Although they expected to find treasure, Chase, Frank, and Griff hid their disappointment. Then, Frank asked, "Do you think we should look at his will, Mr. Rigsby? I know that Miss Margaret has already been awarded the property, but there's no use her searching all around the house if what's here is all there is."

"I don't see what harm there can be in that. And I think we should take this with us and let her attorney and the courts authenticate it."

....

Chase held one of the flashlights and led the group of five as they ascended the staircase. Mr. Rigsby was in the middle and carried the parchment pages. Thomas brought up the rear holding the second flashlight. They carefully navigated the narrow passageway and took care to assist their elderly friend as they climbed the steep steps.

When Chase reached the last section of stairs, he could once again see daylight ahead coming through the bedroom windows. On the second from the final step, he lost his footing and tripped forward. Instinctively he reached out to steady himself, and his hand hit against the wall. That motion caused the mechanism that opened the hidden door panel to trip. With a sickening scrape, the sliding door panel slammed and it latched closed!

"Not good!" said Chase.

"What happened?" Frank asked from the back of the group.

"The door panel just closed on us," Chase said, "and I'm not seeing any handles or any way to open it from this side."

With almost no room on the narrow steps for a second boy to assist, and with no tools available to pry the panel open, all thoughts went to the worst scenario. *We're trapped, and nobody knows we're here!*

....

UP FROM THE DEPTHS

Chapter X

"Fellows," said Mr. Rigsby, "be still where you are and rest for a moment. This is serious, and I want us to pray and ask God for his help. You and I are never out of his sight, and we can always ask for his protection. Bow your heads with me as I speak a prayer. *Father in Heaven, you see us right where we are, and you know what we need. God, we need your help and your creativity to find a way out of here. We will thank you in advance for answering this prayer. Amen.*"

"Thomas, you're the strongest of the five of us," continued Mr. Rigsby, "but there is no way for you to pass the others on these steps to get to the door to push on it."

Chase spoke from the front of the group. "I'm telling you, Mr. Rigsby, it wouldn't help. That door is solid, and there's no place around the edges that I can find for even a fingernail!"

The five of them had been standing for several minutes, but one by one they carefully sat on the steps in silence. Each person's mind was deep in thought; trying to come up with any solution that could help them out of their circumstances.

"Wait a minute," exclaimed Griff. "I have our walkie-talkies in my shoulder bag. The hills are pretty high out here, and maybe I can reach somebody with my radio and get them to send help." As Griff spoke, he was already unzipping his bag and extending the walkie-talkie's antenna to its full position. He switched the radio to its highest power.

"Breaker, breaker! Can anybody hear me? We need some help. We're trapped south of Lewisville on Highway 11. Breaker, breaker!"

He released the transmit button, and everyone held his breath as they waited for someone, *anyone,* to respond.

"Breaker, breaker! Can anybody hear me?"

From the speaker came a familiar voice. "Griff, is that you calling?" It was Kate, Frank's sister.

"Yes, it's me, Kate. Oh, thank goodness you heard me! Five of us are stuck inside a wall at the old Hickory Hill farmhouse south of town! Can you get somebody here quick? Over."

"My goodness, Griff. Yes! I'll call – I'll call somebody! Just hang on. Are you all okay? Just take care of yourselves. We'll get there as fast as possible. I was walking past Frank's room and heard you from his base station radio. I'm not even supposed to be at home right now, but I had to come back to pick up some things for a group project that I'd forgotten. Over."

Frank grabbed Griff's radio. "This is amazing, Kate. We prayed that we'd find a way out of here, and you were the answer! Please give my spare walkie-talkie to whoever comes, or they'll never figure out how to find us. We'll have to talk them through the steps to reach us where we are. Over."

"Okay, Frank. I'm signing off now. You should see some-body within a half-hour. Over and out!"

"Goodbye, sis. Thank you so much! Thank you!"

There was an awe within the staircase as the walkie-talkie went silent. In the quietness, each person considered their perilous situation, the petition spoken by Leonard Rigsby, and the solution only moments later. A very relieved Mr. Rigsby said, "Don't ever let anyone tell you that God isn't listening to our heartfelt prayers."

"Save your batteries, guys," Chase said. "We may still need both of your flashlights before this is all over with."

....

Forty minutes after they last heard from Kate, her voice crackled through the speaker of Griff's walkie-talkie. "We're just now arriving, Frank. Can you still hear me?"

"Loud and clear, and you sure sound great to us! The front door is open, and you're going to want to come to the sec-ond floor. When you get there, go into the first room on the right. It's the master bedroom."

"Okay, we're walking in now."

The sound of muffled footsteps from a distance reached the hidden staircase. Then, footfalls that seemed much closer became louder and suddenly stopped.

"We're inside the room. Where are you?" Kate asked over the walkie-talkie.

"Go into the closet next to the chifferobe," Frank instructed on his radio. "On the wall, you'll see some wooden pegs. Push up on the middle one, the loose one."

Frank had barely finished his explanation when the hidden panel suddenly slid open. Face-to-face with them in the master bedroom were Mr. Whidden, Kate, Reverend Metcalfe, and Miss Margaret Hettinger.

"Don't anyone blame the boys," said Mr. Rigsby as the group emerged from the hidden staircase. "This is all my doing. And Margaret," he continued as he turned to Miss Hettinger showing a mischievous smile and holding up the parchment papers, "I believe we just saved you a lot of searching."

. . . .

While Kate, the three friends, and Mr. Rigsby sat on the front porch, they talked about the events of the last hour. The others descended the secret steps and returned with the wooden boxes from below. They carried them into the dining room and pried open their lids.

Mr. Whidden called for those waiting on the porch to join them. The men and Miss Hettinger had spread out the contents from the boxes on the large table. Those wooden boxes held numerous deeds and official documents. Some were bearer bonds issued by railroads, while others were stock certificates of petroleum companies, and municipal bonds.

The third box, the heaviest of them all, contained a handwritten note that was signed by Mr. Hettinger. Beneath the note were small containers filled with hundreds of rare, proof coins from United States Mints across the country.

Margaret Hettinger took several minutes to examine their contents, then read to the group from the note. *"It is my wish that the value of these coins be used specifically to provide shelter, provisions, and education for those less fortunate than I have been."* She turned to those assembled in the room and said, "This will be the first thing I shall do. I believe I'll be able to accomplish something very nice in my uncle's honor for many deserving people in our area."

After a thoughtful pause, Miss Hettinger turned to Griff, Chase, and Frank and hugged each one. "Thank you, boys, for making this search so much easier."

"Let's all go back to town," Mr. Whidden said. "You five have had quite an afternoon. If anybody's interested, Fazelli's Ice Cream Bar has added three new flavors to their menu, and I'm buying!"

....

The rescue party and the ones who were rescued pushed three tables together at Fazelli's. Mr. Whidden ordered milkshakes for all in the group.

While they waited on their orders, Leonard Rigsby spoke. "You three boys have great perception to notice the way those bedrooms differed. And then to learn that the secret room contained so many things of value! Do you recall that Bible verse you boys asked me about? It said that where our treasure is, our hearts are found there, too. It seems that the treasure of Hickory Hill was located in the very *heart* of the house; at its foundation!"

"Hey, Chase," said Thomas from the end of the table. "What's your last name?"

"It's Spencer," Chase replied.

"Did you ever have a metal flashlight with your name engraved along the barrel?"

After a long pause, Chase exclaimed, "That was *you*? That was *your* backpack in the storm drain, and it was *you* that we saw coming out of the opening?"

With mischief in his voice, Thomas replied, "Guilty on all counts!"

"We thought that the three of us were the only ones who went into the storm drains, but you did, too!" Frank said.

"Yes, but not because I wanted to," Thomas replied. "When I first got into town I had *no* place to sleep. I spent the nights for almost two weeks near the cemetery sleeping in the drainpipes. I didn't know a soul. What you didn't realize, Griff, is that when I came to your church and you served me that lunch and seemed to care about me, for the very first time I felt that maybe I was going to make it."

Thomas looked into the faces of the people around the table starting with Reverend Metcalfe. "Thanks to you and your church, and you, Mr. Rigsby, and you three guys, I now have some real friendships – and I have hope again for my future."

"Welcome to your new family!" Kate said with a smile.

Griff turned to Thomas, patted him on the back and said, "Yeah, it's good to have another stormdrain rat on the team!"

"Thomas," Chase asked, "you wanna' go sewer-stomping after we finish here?"

"No way, no how!" Thomas muttered, shaking his head. All of those seated around the table broke into loud laughter.

Lay not up for yourselves treasures upon earth, where moth and rust doth corrupt, and where thieves break through and steal: but lay up for yourselves treasures in heaven, where neither moth nor rust doth corrupt, and where thieves do not break through nor steal:
for where your treasure is,
there will your heart be also.
Matthew 6:19-21

You are a treasure!

Chase, Griff, Frank, Thomas, and Mr. Rigsby discovered lots of valuable things at the bottom of the secret staircase. It must have been very exciting to see the shiny coins that came from the wooden box they found down below. Frank's father, Miss Margaret, and Reverend Metcalfe spread them out on the table inside of the Hickory Hill farmhouse. I can't imagine how awesome that was!

You and I might never touch or even see a treasure like that one, but you need to know this one thing: In God's eyes you are worth more than a chest full of silver or gold – MUCH more!

It doesn't matter the size of your house, the price tag on your mom's or dad's car; whether you are tall or short; wear the cool shoes or second-hand clothes, God loves you exactly like you are because He created you, and He made you perfect!

If you ever get discouraged or your friends let you down, remember that nothing can separate you from God's love. His love reaches you in happy times and in the sad, dark places.

The Bible tells us that Jesus is the friend that sticks closer than a brother (or a sister)! Just call out to Him (in prayer) when you need Him, and He will meet you wherever you are!

Enjoy other books in the
Bon Air Boys Adventures series

"Lights On Wildcat Mountain"

"Whispers In The Wind"

and more...

Available as eBooks or through *Audible*

The Bon Air Boys

Chase, Griff, and Frank

Made in the USA
Columbia, SC
26 February 2020